Green Light Readers

For the new reader who's ready to GO!

Amazing adventures await every young child who is eager to read.
Green Light Readers encourage children to explore, to imagine, and to grow
through books. Created for beginning readers at two levels of skill, these lively illustrated
stories have been carefully developed to reinforce reading basics taught at school and
to make reading a fun and rewarding experience for children and grown-ups to share
outside the classroom.

The grades and ages within each skill level are general guidelines only, and books
included in both levels may feature any or all of the bulleted characteristics. When
choosing a book for a new reader, remember that every child progresses at his or her
own pace—be patient and supportive as the magic of reading takes hold.

1 Buckle up!
Kindergarten–Grade 1: Developing reading skills, ages 5–7
- Short, simple stories • Fully illustrated • Familiar objects and situations
- Playful rhythms • Spoken language patterns of children
- Rhymes and repeated phrases • Strong link between text and art

2 Start the engine!
Grades 1–2: Reading with help, ages 6–8
- Longer stories, including nonfiction • Short chapters
- Generously illustrated • Less-familiar situations
- More fully developed characters • Creative language, including dialogue
- More subtle link between text and art

*Green Light Readers incorporate characteristics detailed in the Reading Recovery model
used by educators to assess the readability of texts through the end of first grade.
Guidelines for reading levels for these readers have been developed with assistance from
Mary Lou Meerson. An educational consultant, Ms. Meerson has been a classroom teacher,
a language arts coordinator, an elementary school principal, and a university professor.*

Published in collaboration with Harcourt School Publishers

10 WASHINGTON PARK

Digger Pig
and the
Turnip

Digger Pig
and the
Turnip

Caron Lee Cohen
Illustrated by Christopher Denise

Green Light Readers
Harcourt, Inc.
San Diego   New York   London

First Green Light Readers edition 2000
Green Light Readers is a registered trademark of Harcourt, Inc.

Library of Congress Cataloging-in-Publication Data
Cohen, Caron Lee.
Digger Pig and the turnip/Caron Lee Cohen; illustrated by Christopher Denise.
—1st Green Light Readers ed.
p. cm.
"Green Light Readers."
Summary: In this adaptation of a traditional folktale, a dog, duck, and chick refuse
to help a pig prepare a turnip pie but nevertheless expect to eat it when it's ready.
[1. Folklore.] I. Denise, Christopher, ill. II. Title.
PZ8.1.C66455Di 2000
398.24'52—dc21 99-6802
ISBN 0-15-202524-3
ISBN 0-15-202530-8 (pb)

A C E G H F D B

A C E G H F D B (pb)

One day Digger Pig dug up a big turnip.
"I can use this to make a good turnip pie,"
she said.

Chirper Chick, Quacker Duck, and Bow-Wow Dog sat around in their corner of the barn.

"Let's make a turnip pie," said Digger Pig. "Who will help me cut the turnip?"

"Not I," said Chirper Chick.
"Not I," said Quacker Duck.
"Not I," said Bow-Wow Dog.

"All right then. I will cut the turnip myself," said Digger Pig.

And she did.

Then Digger Pig asked, "Who will help me mash the turnip?"

"Not I," said Chirper Chick.
"Not I," said Quacker Duck.
"Not I," said Bow-Wow Dog.

"All right then. I will mash the turnip myself," said Digger Pig.

And she did.

Next, Digger Pig asked, "Who
will help me make the pie?"

"Not I," said Chirper Chick.
"Not I," said Quacker Duck.
"Not I," said Bow-Wow Dog.

"All right then. I will make the pie myself!" said Digger Pig.

And she did.
She called her piglets to supper.

"Can we have some pie?" the others asked.
"No!" grunted Digger Pig. "You didn't
help. My piglets and I will eat it all."

And they did!

Meet the Illustrator

Christopher Denise likes drawing animals. Before he starts to draw, he looks at pictures of real animals to get ideas. He says, "I know children will like a story even more if the animals are really special."

Christopher Denise

Look for these other Green Light Readers
in affordably priced paperbacks and hardcovers!

Green Light Readers
For the new reader who's ready to GO!